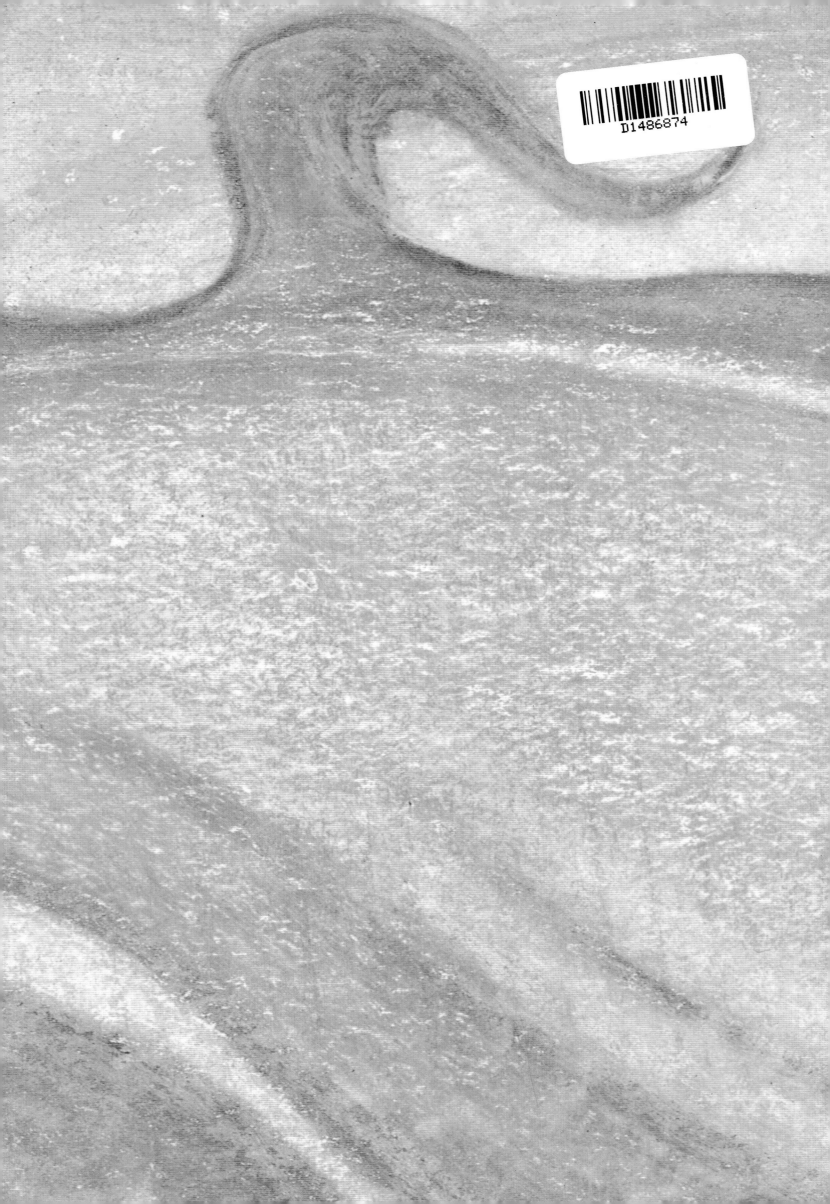

First U.S. Edition 1995

ISBN 0-316-50361-4

Library of Congress Catalog Card Number 94-73193

10 9 8 7 6 5 4 3 2 1

Printed in Spain

The Cranky Sun

Jerry Kramsky ♦ Lorenzo Mattotti

Little, Brown and Company
Boston   New York   Toronto   London

Once upon a time there was a little village named Underwind, where fantastic things happened. Underwind was famous, for it had two extraordinary attractions. There was its garden of sweets, and…

In the middle of the village was a special clock. It was at the very top of a tower where everyone could see it. TICK-TICK-TICK; it never missed a stroke. The villagers believed that the clock controlled the sun, for when the clock said noon, the sun was overhead, and when the clock struck midnight, the sun was always gone.

But one day something went wrong. The clock chimed the nighttime hours as usual, but the sun…well, looking very cranky, she stayed up in the middle of the sky.

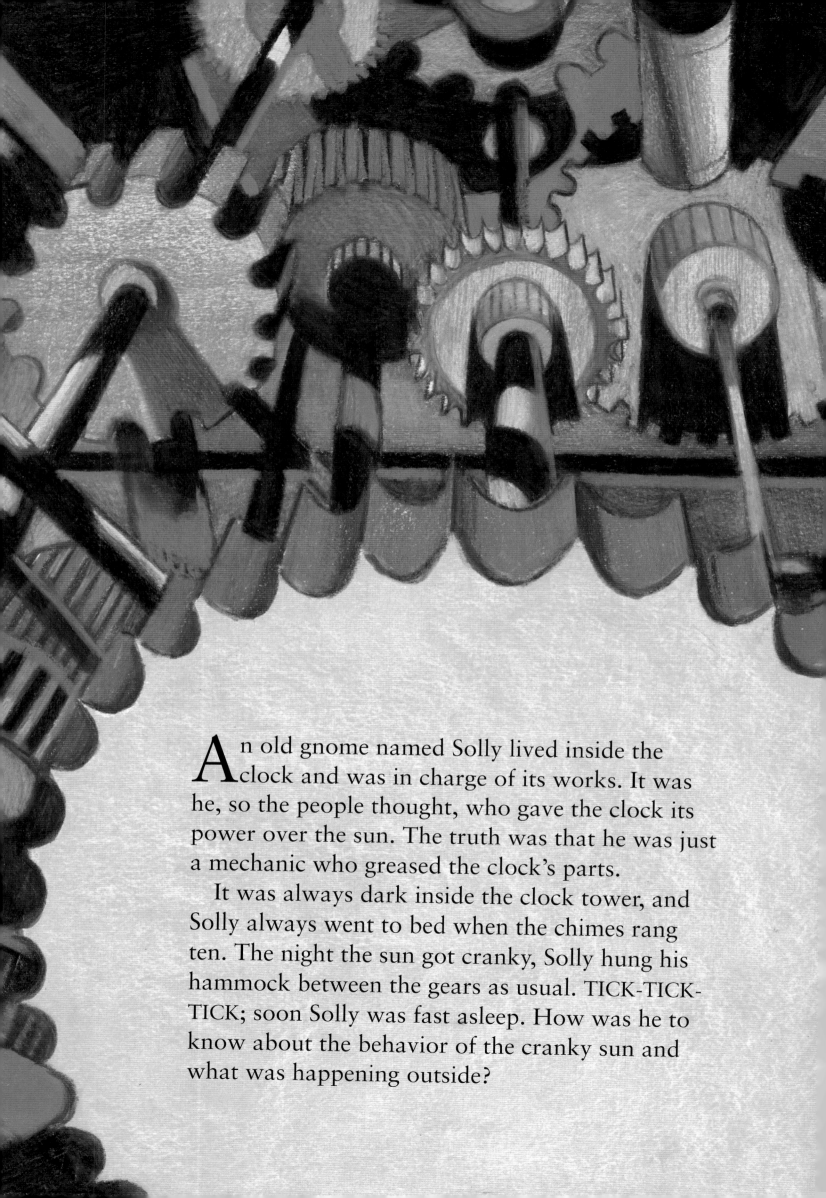

An old gnome named Solly lived inside the clock and was in charge of its works. It was he, so the people thought, who gave the clock its power over the sun. The truth was that he was just a mechanic who greased the clock's parts.

It was always dark inside the clock tower, and Solly always went to bed when the chimes rang ten. The night the sun got cranky, Solly hung his hammock between the gears as usual. TICK-TICK-TICK; soon Solly was fast asleep. How was he to know about the behavior of the cranky sun and what was happening outside?

In the streets, however, everyone was worried. "Look at the sun! What's she doing up at this hour?"

"Hey, what's going on?"

Although it was now midnight, the sun shone brighter than ever. The grown-ups, who were not used to this sort of thing, grumbled to themselves. The children, on the other hand, up past their bedtimes, were very excited and ran about overjoyed.

That same night an old vagabond arrived in the city. All his life he had lived in parks and fed the birds he found there. He had become so friendly with the birds that he even learned their language. As he was sitting under a tree on that brilliant evening, a seagull landed in an overhead branch and said, "It's all very strange. The sun, for some reason, has gotten cranky and absolutely refuses to go to sleep. She says she won't take orders from the clock anymore. What does she mean? It's crazy."

The vagabond got up and ran to tell the mayor what he had heard.

The townspeople began to panic.
A day that lasted and lasted…
surely that could not be right. The town
would get too hot! When would anyone
get a good night's sleep? The mayor
called a meeting. Someone must be
found to reason with this cranky sun.

The first one to try was Polo-Pom-Pom, the noted composer and singer. Accompanied by violins, guitars, and lutes, Polo-Pom-Pom sang out to the sun, "Listen, Miss Sun, you're making me sad. I sing about moonlight in every song. With you here, the moon won't appear, and, my dear, that is wrong. Go to bed, Miss Sun, and make me glad."

But the sun stayed put in the sky. Perhaps she didn't hear him. Perhaps, with reason, she didn't like his song.

When they heard the word *moon* in the song, everyone started thinking of astronauts. So they called in a team of space explorers. Like acrobats, the astronauts hurled themselves toward the sun.

They called out, "Hey, you, Sun! You must go to bed. With you around we can't see the stars. How will we navigate?"

The sun replied, "More orders! Hmpph," and only glowed brighter. The astronauts, afraid of getting burned, returned to the town, defeated.

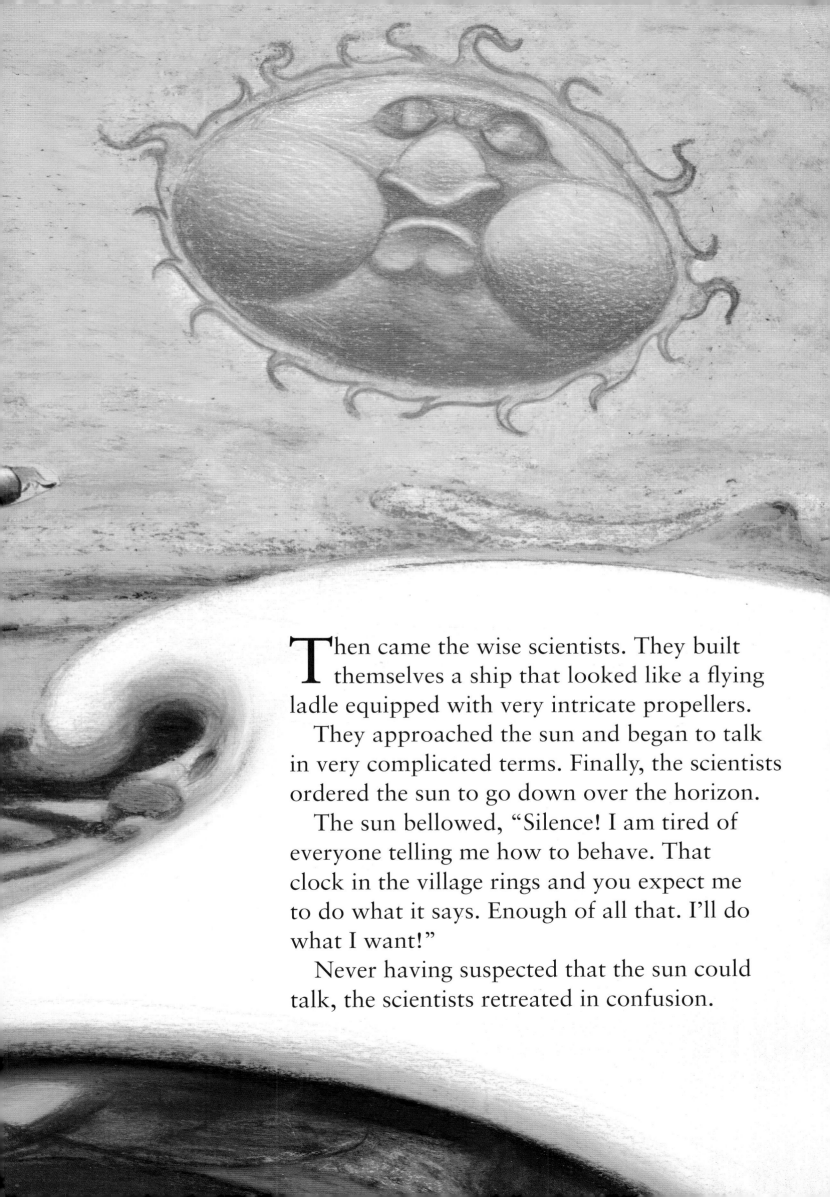

Then came the wise scientists. They built themselves a ship that looked like a flying ladle equipped with very intricate propellers.

They approached the sun and began to talk in very complicated terms. Finally, the scientists ordered the sun to go down over the horizon.

The sun bellowed, "Silence! I am tired of everyone telling me how to behave. That clock in the village rings and you expect me to do what it says. Enough of all that. I'll do what I want!"

Never having suspected that the sun could talk, the scientists retreated in confusion.

Who could reason with the sun? The local poet tried. He had such a long neck that it was said he lived with his head in the clouds; obviously he would be the perfect one to approach the sun. He attempted in his mild way to write a poem begging the sun to set. Unless she went to bed, people couldn't sleep anymore, and all dreams would disappear. He became so overwhelmed with sadness that he began to cry and never finished the poem.

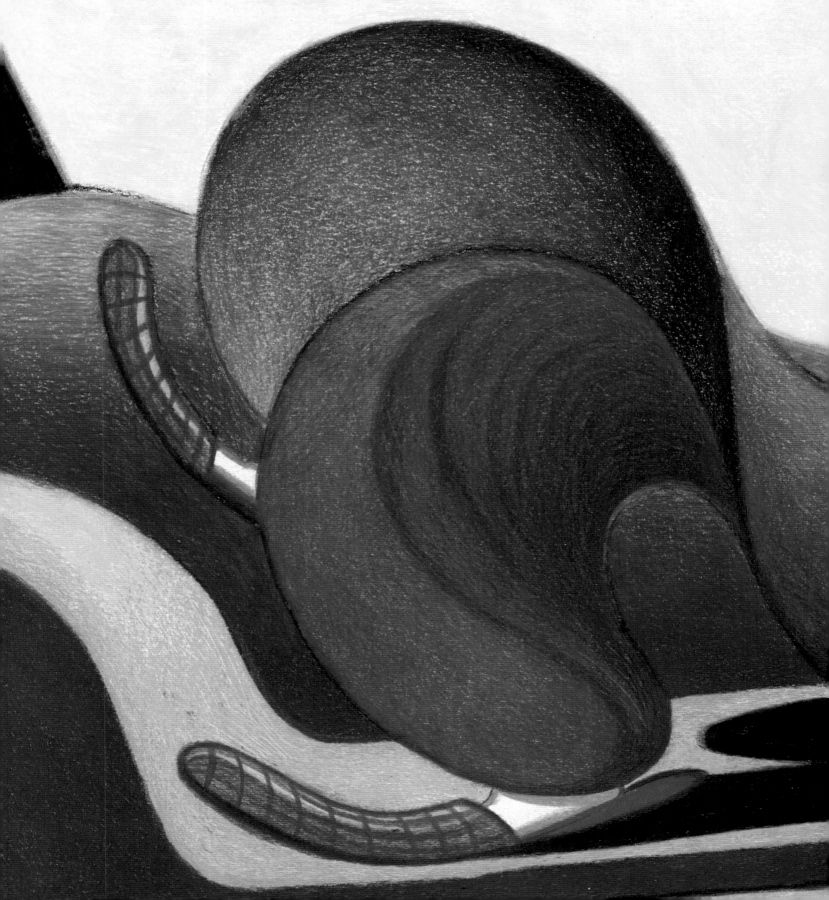

The town robbers were the most upset of anyone. With so much light in the sky, how could they hide in the shadows and steal from people? Really, the situation with this cranky sun was getting to be most impossible!

In desperation, the town called on a man who claimed he could train the clouds. He was a fantastic character with a winged whip. He said that if the sun would not set, he would train all the clouds to gather in front of her and block her rays. Alas, it turned out he was a faker. The clouds went on their way, blowing across the sky, and paid him no attention at all.

Eventually all the people in town tried their own solutions.
The local cook, for example, offered the sun a wonderful
meal of seasoned spaghetti if only she would go to sleep over
the horizon. Nothing worked.

But in the end it was really quite simple. One day a small boy on his way home from playing yet another long, hot game of ball looked up at the sun. "I'm really tired," he said. "I'd like to go home, hear a story, and go to bed." He rubbed his eyes and glanced at the sun. "You must be tired, too, huh?"

That's all it took. No one had ordered the sun to do anything. No one had rung a chime and expected the sun to be in a certain place at a certain time. A little boy was tired and thought the sun might be tired, too. Hearing his gentle suggestion, the sun realized that staying up so long *had* exhausted her. Within an hour she stopped being cranky and went to bed. The townsfolk were surprised and full of wonder. Why had the sun decided to set? Had someone said a magic word?

The little boy slipped into bed and was soon fast asleep in his darkened room. The stars came out and shone through his window. The constellations were brilliant and easy to pick out, but where was the moon? Could it be possible that he was refusing to rise and glow?

Ah, but that is another story altogether.

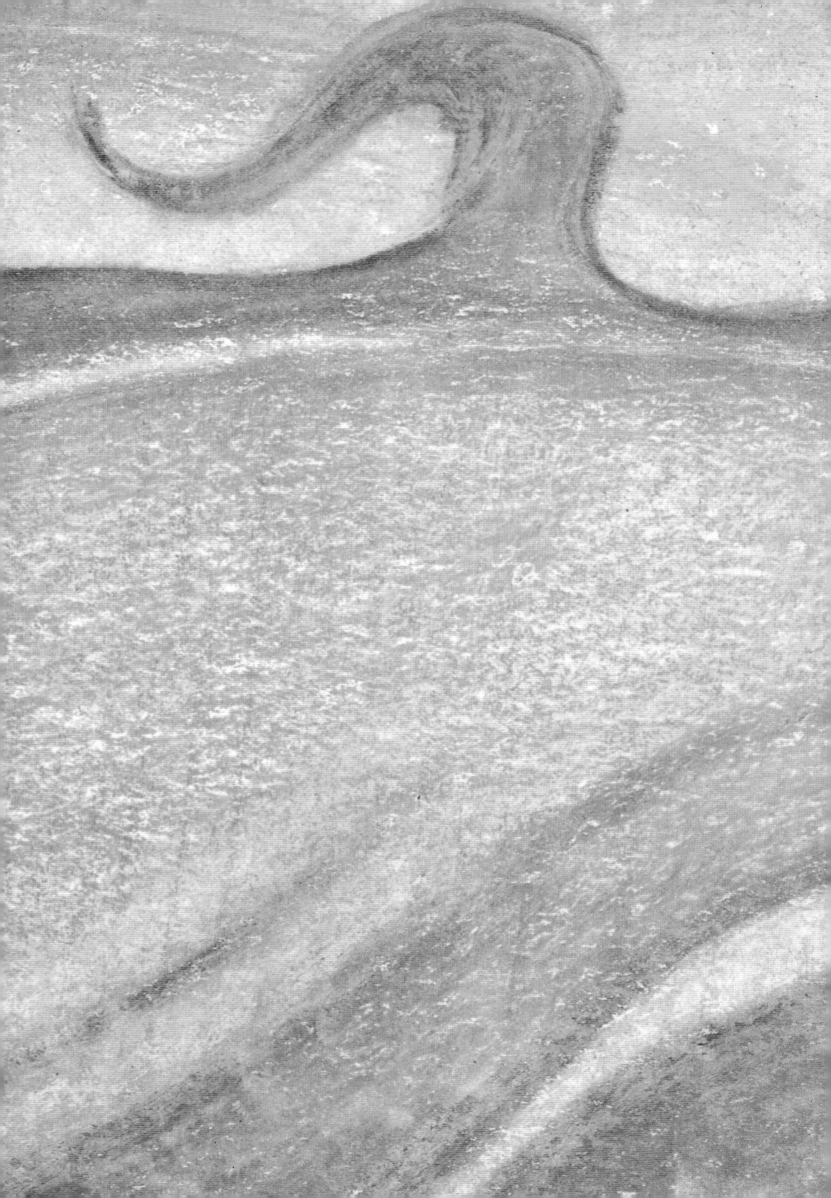